Temple Israel Library
Minneapolis, Minn.

———

Please sign your full name on the above card.

Return books promptly to the Library or Temple Office.

Fines will be charged for overdue books or for damage or loss of same.

DEMCO

HONI'S CIRCLE OF TREES

by Phillis Gershator
illustrated by Mim Green

The Jewish Publication Society / Philadelphia and Jerusalem / 5755 / 1994

Library of Congress Cataloging–in–Publication Data

Gershator, Phillis.
Honi's circle of trees / Phillis Gershator;
illustrated by Mim Green.
p. cm.
A retelling of: Honi and his magic circle.
Summary: Retells the wondrous deeds of Honi the Circle Maker who wandered
over the land of ancient Israel planting carob seeds.
ISBN 0–8276–0511–0

1. Ḥoni, ha-Me'aggel, 1st cent. B.C.—Juvenile literature. 2. Talmud—Biography—Juvenile literature. 3.
Jews—Folklore. 4. Legends, Jewish. [1. Ḥoni, ha-Me'aggel, 1st cent. B.C. 2. Jews—Biography.
3. Folklore, Jewish.] I. Green, Mim, ill. II. Gershator, Phillis. Honi and his magic circle. III. Title.
BM530.H66G48 1994
296 1'2'0092—dc20
[B]

93–29748 ✓
CIP
AC

Designed by Helene Krasney

10 9 8 7 6 5 4 3 2 1

In memoriam, Abraham Gershator, story-teller.

To David Gershator for the inspirational touches

and to May Garelick and Bruce Black

for the finishing touches.

— P.G. and M.G.

I n the hills of ancient Israel, there lived a man called Honi. Honi was a wanderer and a doer of good deeds, and on his back he carried a sack. The sack was filled with carobs, shiny brown fruit picked from trees his grandfather had planted many years ago.

When the carobs were freshly picked, they were soft and juicy and sweet as honey. As the days passed, they became hard and dry, and the smooth seeds rattled inside. But even after the carobs grew dry, they were sweet and good and stayed that way for a long, long time.

Honi ate dry carobs from his sack. Then he planted the seeds. He planted carob seeds wherever he wandered over the land of Israel.

And so it was that all across the hills and valleys, from Judea to Galilee, from the Big Sea to the Great Desert, sturdy carob trees spread their branches.

Honi's trees bore fruit for man and beast—food for the traveler, sweets for the children, and fodder for the animals.

Honi loved animals. And the animals, even wild creatures, loved Honi.

When he stopped to rest in the evening, the animals gathered around him. The wild, howling jackal laid its head on Honi's lap and yelped happily like a puppy. Shy gazelles nuzzled up to him and nibbled carobs from his hand. Sparrows settled on his shoulder. Swallows swooped and circled overhead. Snakes and scorpions nestled at his feet. And while he slept, the animals stood guard.

One Friday, as the Sabbath drew close, Honi came to a village in a valley. The villagers welcomed him, inviting him to pray with them and to share their Sabbath feast. After the Sabbath, when the evening stars twinkled in the sky and the candles burned low, Honi and the villagers sang songs and told stories late into the night.

In the morning, Honi was on his way again, planting carobs.

That same day, a man from the village and his children stopped
to watch Honi.

"Hello, old man. What are you planting?"

"Carob seeds," Honi answered.

"How long will it take for the trees to bear fruit?"
asked the man.

"Seventy years," Honi said.

"Seventy years! Do you expect to pick the fruit?"

"Of course not," said Honi. "I will not be alive in seventy years. But my forefathers planted trees that bear fruit for us, and now I am planting trees for those to come, those I will never see."

"My children and grandchildren will remember your good deeds," said the man. "What is your name?"

"Honi."

"The Honi
 they call
 Ha-Me'aggel,
 the Circle Maker?"

"Yes."

"Ah! Honi the Circle Maker!" exclaimed the man. "I know of your magic. When you stand in the middle of your magic circle, you can ask the Lord for anything, even rain. I remember once, when the cisterns were dry and the earth was as hard as clay, you brought rain to my own village."

"But now, Honi Ha-Me'aggel,
the midday sun is high.
You must not work
too long and hard
in the hot sun."

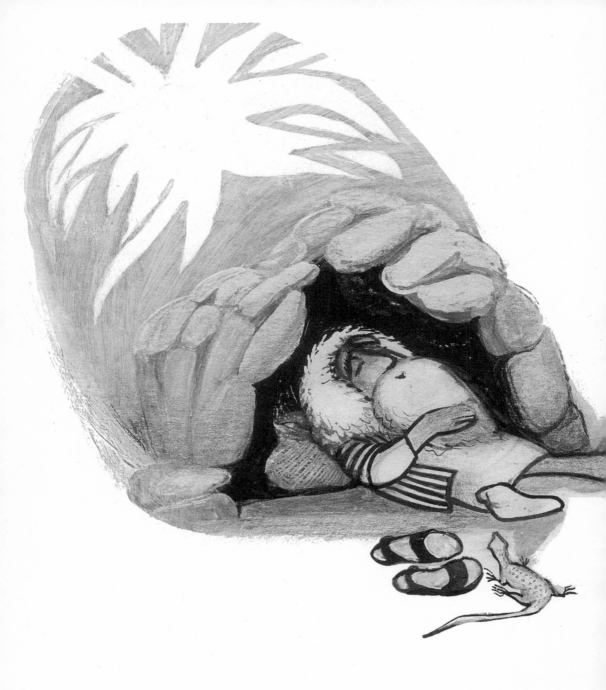

Honi took the man's advice. He lay down behind some rocks to rest.
The rocks felt cool, and Honi closed his eyes.

As he drifted off to sleep, a cloud settled over him. It seemed to carry him away — higher than the snows of Mount Hermon, higher than the migrating storks flying over land and sea.

While Honi slept, the sun rose and set
more times than one can count. Old stars exploded
and new stars shimmered in the skies. While Honi slept,
generations were born and generations died.

While Honi slept, the Torah, read from the beginning to end every year, was read over and over seventy times.

When Honi awoke,
the cloud melted away like the dew.

He heard voices calling, "Carob! Sweet carob!"

Honi sat up to see men, women, and children picking carobs off a
nearby tree. He rubbed his eyes and stretched. His beard was longer
and whiter than he remembered, his clothes older and mustier,
his carob sack in shreds.

"I don't remember seeing this beautiful tree before," Honi said.

"It was planted in the days of Honi Ha-Me'aggel," a man replied.

"But I am Honi Ha-Me'aggel."

"Oh, no! Honi died a long, long time ago. The sun must be too hot for you. Why don't you sit here in the shade and try to remember who you are?"

"I *am* Honi Ha-Me'aggel," Honi repeated.
"I was planting carob seeds just yesterday.
I spoke to a man and his children and then lay down behind
the rocks and fell asleep."

"Come with us, old man," said the carob pickers. "Come home with us."

The children let Honi ride their little white donkey.

Swaying on the donkey's back, he looked curiously this way and that until they came to a village. It was the village in the valley, but many of the buildings were faded and falling apart. Many others were new and brightly painted.

"Could they have been built in a day and a night," he wondered, "while I slept?"

When they reached the synagogue, Honi stopped to say his daily prayers. He expected to see his old friends. He hoped they might be able to explain the day's strange events. But Honi didn't recognize any of the men in the synagogue."Where is Saul the Weaver?" Honi asked.

"Who?"

"Where is Uriel the Carpenter?"

"Who?"

"Avram the Shoemaker? Where is he?"

"Who? Are you in the wrong town, old man?"

One of the men spoke up. "I knew Saul, Uriel, and Avram when I was young, but they died many years ago. What did you say your name is?"

"Honi Ha-Me'aggel."

"Honi Ha-Me'aggel!" exclaimed the man. "But that is impossible! I met him when I was a child, more than seventy years ago. Even then he was a very old man. He told my father he was planting carobs."

"I am Honi Ha-Me'aggel," said Honi, "and I plant carobs."

"How can that be?
   Doesn't he know who he is?" the villagers asked one another.

They thought Honi was making up stories.

Honi was so sad, he walked
away and drew a circle on the ground.

He stood in the middle of the circle and said,
"Oh Lord, I never bothered You with my own problems,
but the people do not believe that I am Honi Ha-Me'aggel.
Why did You let me live beyond my time?
Why didn't You take me while I rested by the rocks?"

Honi bowed his head in sorrow.

All of a sudden the truth came to him. He lifted his head, and tears of joy sparkled in his eyes.

"Now I understand!" he cried. "You have given me a gift few receive. Thank You, Lord. Thank You! You have allowed me to see my trees bear fruit!"

Honi drew his last circle in the ground. It grew larger and larger,
ringing the land with its magic.

And Honi's circle keeps growing, wherever people

plant trees for their children and grandchildren.